Night Owl

Anders Hanson

Illustrated by Anne Haberstroh

Consulting Editor, Diane Craig, M.A./Reading Specialist

Published by ABDO Publishing Company, 4940 Viking Drive, Edina, Minnesota 55435.

Printed in the United States.

Credits
Edited by: Pam Price
Curriculum Coordinator: Nancy Tuminelly
Cover and Interior Design and Production: Mighty Media
Photo Credits: Corbis Images, Digital Vision, Eyewire Images, John Foxx, Marco Mastrorilli, ShutterStock

Library of Congress Cataloging-in-Publication Data

Hanson, Anders, 1980-
    Night Owl / Anders Hanson ; illustrated by Anne Haberstroh.
        p. cm. -- (Fact & fiction. Animal tales)
    Summary: Opa, the first owl, visits the moon and learns many wonderful secrets, but when he tries to tell his friends back on Earth about them, all he can say is "hoo." Includes facts about owls.
    ISBN 1-59679-953-6 (hardcover)
    ISBN 1-59679-954-4 (paperback)
    [1. Owls--Fiction. 2. Moon--Fiction. 3. Speech--Fiction.] I. Haberstroh, Anne, ill. II. Title. III. Series.

    PZ7.H1982867Nig 2006
    [E]--dc22

                                                                                            2005027836

SandCastle Level: Fluent

SandCastle™ books are created by a professional team of educators, reading specialists, and content developers around five essential components—phonemic awareness, phonics, vocabulary, text comprehension, and fluency—to assist young readers as they develop reading skills and strategies and increase their general knowledge. All books are written, reviewed, and leveled for guided reading, early reading intervention, and Accelerated Reader® programs for use in shared, guided, and independent reading and writing activities to support a balanced approach to literacy instruction. The SandCastle™ series has four levels that correspond to early literacy development. The levels help teachers and parents select appropriate books for young readers.

| **Emerging Readers** | **Beginning Readers** | **Transitional Readers** | **Fluent Readers** |
| (no flags) | (1 flag) | (2 flags) | (3 flags) |

These levels are meant only as a guide. All levels are subject to change.

FACT & FiCTiON

This series provides early fluent readers the opportunity to develop reading comprehension strategies and increase fluency. These books are appropriate for guided, shared, and independent reading.

FACT The left-hand pages incorporate realistic photographs to enhance readers' understanding of informational text.

FiCTiON The right-hand pages engage readers with an entertaining, narrative story that is supported by whimsical illustrations.

The Fact and Fiction pages can be read separately to improve comprehension through questioning, predicting, making inferences, and summarizing. They can also be read side-by-side, in spreads, which encourages students to explore and examine different writing styles.

FACT OR FiCTiON? This fun quiz helps reinforce students' understanding of what is real and not real.

SPEED READ The text-only version of each section includes word-count rulers for fluency practice and assessment.

GLOSSARY Higher-level vocabulary and concepts are defined in the glossary.

SandCastle™ would like to hear from you.

Tell us your stories about reading this book. What was your favorite page? Was there something hard that you needed help with? Share the ups and downs of learning to read. To get posted on the ABDO Publishing Company Web site, send us an e-mail at:

sandcastle@abdopublishing.com

Owls have existed for about 60 million years.

A long time ago, when animals still ruled the planet, there lived an owl named Opa. Opa was a magnificent owl. In fact, he was the first owl. But unlike his grandchildren that live with us today, Opa liked to fly under the light of the sun.

5

Owls have the best hearing of any bird.
Owls can locate and catch their prey
through sound alone.

Opa could fly higher, see farther, hear better, and sing more beautifully than any bird in the forest. His only teacher was the wind itself.

Owls have large, broad wings and relatively small bodies. This allows them to glide easily through the air without spending much energy flapping their wings.

One day, the wind
noticed Opa flying so high
that he almost touched the
moon. The wind warned
Opa not to go to the moon.
"Things that go to the
moon never return the
same," he said.

Because owls fly so effortlessly, they are able to remain aloft for long periods of time.

That evening, while the rest of the animals slept, Opa ignored the wind's warning and flew to the moon. The moon was truly happy to see Opa. "Oh, thank you for visiting me, Opa," said the moon. "I'm ever so lonely up here. Would you stay with me a while?"

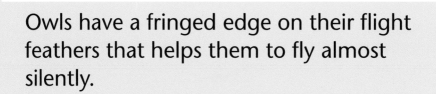

Owls have a fringed edge on their flight feathers that helps them to fly almost silently.

So Opa stayed with the moon all
night long, and the wise old moon
taught him many things. She taught
Opa to fly without a sound and to
see clearly in the dark of night.

13

In some cultures, the owl represents wisdom. In others cultures, it represents trickery and evil.

When morning came and it was time for the moon to be on her way, she told Opa one last thing, "These gifts I have given you cannot be shared with your friends on Earth. If you speak of these things, your voice will only make one sound, and your friends will think you are crazy."

Although owls are best known for their hooting, they are able to make a great variety of noises.

When Opa returned to Earth, he forgot all about the moon's warning. He tried to tell the other birds about the moon's incredible wisdom, but all that came out was hoo, hoo, h-hoo.

Most owls are nocturnal. They sleep during the day and become active at night.

Unable to share his knowledge, Opa retreated into the night where he and the moon kept each other company. Even today, on a clear, quiet night, you may hear his grandchildren still trying to share their secrets with you, but all they can say is hoo, hoo, h-hoo.

FACT or Fiction?

Read each statement below. Then decide whether it's from the FACT section or the Fiction section!

  1. Owls are able to fly for long periods of time.

 2. Owls have excellent hearing.

  3. Owls can only make one kind of sound.

  4. Owls can fly to the moon.

Owls have existed for about 60 million years. 8

Owls have the best hearing of any bird. Owls can 18
locate and catch their prey through sound alone. 26

Owls have large, broad wings and relatively small 34
bodies. This allows them to glide easily through the air 44
without spending much energy flapping their wings. 51

Because owls fly so effortlessly, they are able to 60
remain aloft for long periods of time. 67

Owls have a fringed edge on their flight feathers 76
that helps them to fly almost silently. 83

In some cultures, the owl represents wisdom. In 91
others cultures, it represents trickery and evil. 98

Although owls are best known for their hooting, 106
they are able to make a great variety of noises. 116

Most owls are nocturnal. They sleep during the day 125
and become active at night. 130

A long time ago, when animals still ruled the   9
planet, there lived an owl named Opa. Opa was   18
a magnificent owl. In fact, he was the first owl.   28
But unlike his grandchildren that live with us   36
today, Opa liked to fly under the light of the sun.   47

Opa could fly higher, see farther, hear better,   55
and sing more beautifully than any bird in the   64
forest. His only teacher was the wind itself.   72

One day, the wind noticed Opa flying so high   81
that he almost touched the moon. The wind   89
warned Opa not to go to the moon. "Things that   99
go to the moon never return the same," he said.   109

That evening, while the rest of the animals   117
slept, Opa ignored the wind's warning and flew   125
to the moon. The moon was truly happy to see   135
Opa. "Oh, thank you for visiting me, Opa," said   144
the moon. "I'm ever so lonely up here. Would   153
you stay with me a while?"   159

So Opa stayed with the moon all night long, and 169
the wise old moon taught him many things. She 178
taught Opa to fly without a sound and to see 188
clearly in the dark of night. 194

When morning came and it was time for the 203
moon to be on her way, she told Opa one last 214
thing, "These gifts I have given you cannot be 223
shared with your friends on Earth. If you speak of 233
these things, your voice will only make one sound, 242
and your friends will think you are crazy." 250

When Opa returned to Earth, he forgot all about 259
the moon's warning. He tried to tell the other birds 269
about the moon's incredible wisdom, but all that 277
came out was hoo, hoo, h-hoo. 283

Unable to share his knowledge, Opa retreated into 291
the night where he and the moon kept each other 301
company. Even today, on a clear, quiet night, you may 311
hear his grandchildren still trying to share their secrets 320
with you, but all they can say is hoo, hoo, h-hoo. 331

GLOSSARY

aloft. in a high place

culture. the behavior, beliefs, art, and other products of a particular group of people

magnificent. the best of its kind, grand in appearance

nocturnal. most active at night

prey. an animal that is hunted or caught for food

represent. to stand for or symbolize something else

wisdom. the ability to judge what is right or true based on one's experience, knowledge, and common sense

To see a complete list of SandCastle™ books and other nonfiction titles from ABDO Publishing Company, visit **www.abdopublishing.com** or contact us at: 4940 Viking Drive, Edina, Minnesota 55435 • 1-800-800-1312 • fax: 1-952-831-1632